Flyaway Girl

FLYAWAY GIRL

ANN GRIFALCONI

Little, Brown and Company
Boston   Toronto   London

The author gratefully acknowledges permission to use portions of photographs from the following:

"Africa's Gentle Giants," *National Geographic* (September 1977). Photograph copyright © by Thomas Nebbia. "Hawaii's Far-Flung Paradise," *National Geographic* (September 1977). Photograph copyright © by Jonathan Blair/Woodlin Camp, Inc. *National Geographic*. Photographs copyright © by *National Geographic Magazine*, Washington, D.C. *Nuba*, published by Harper and Row Inc., 1973. Photographs copyright © by Leni Riefenstahl. *African Ark* (p. 130), published by Harry N. Abrams Inc., 1990. Photograph copyright © by Carol Beckwith and Angela Fisher. "Zebras in Field," *Smithsonian* (May 1987). Photograph copyright © by Peter Poulides.

The ancestor chant is loosely based on an African chant cited by Birago Diop in his story "Sarzan," translated for *Modern African Stories*, Fontana Books, 1971. Edited by Charles R. Larson.

First Edition

Library of Congress Cataloging-in-Publication Data

Grifalconi, Ann.
Flyaway girl / Ann Grifalconi. — 1st ed.
  p.   cm.
Summary: Sent by her mother to the edge of the Niger to gather rushes for the Ceremony of Beginnings, Nsia encounters many distractions, until the ancestors' spirits guide her on her way to becoming a wise little woman.
ISBN 0-316-32866-9
[1. Africa — Fiction. 2. Responsibility — Fiction.] I. Title
PZ7.G8813F1   1992
[E] — dc20   90-39799

10 9 8 7 6 5 4 3 2 1

Color separations made by SFERA

Text set in ITC Bookman Light and Medium by Litho Composition Company, Inc. and display lines set in Neuland Inline by Litho Composition Company, Inc.

Printed and bound by New Interlitho

Published simultaneously in Canada by Little, Brown & Company (Canada) Limited

Printed in Italy

Dedicated to my own ancestor spirit in the waters
about my island: my wise and loving mother

"Here comes *Flyaway Girl!*" Nsia's mother would laugh whenever her long-legged daughter would come into view, running up the well-beaten path from the stream below the village. "She will not be here long — she will fly away!"

But her mother was not worried about Nsia straying too far, for in the high village of Sama, which lay on a small branch of the great Niger River, one could see far into the distance.

Sounds carried far, too: mothers could always hear the laughter of their children as they played in the stream that curved about the village.

And they could also hear the sound of their men calling, urging the oxen that pulled the plows. For the farmers of Sama preferred the ancient ways — not for them the noisy machines! There was only the snapping of the whip and the happy barking of the little dogs as they ran alongside.

And always, when they heard the singing of the wind in the trees, the wise mothers knew that the ancestor spirits were there, keeping watch over all . . .

And here at home, where the good smells of cooking mixed with the thick smell of the *banco* (the dried clay mixed with rotten straw that made the houses rainproof), the *Wise Young Matrons* and the *Wise Old Women* gathered at the round cook house and talked and gossiped while preparing the food, often with the help of the older children.

"But now," looking at the rounding form of Nsia's mother, one of the *Wise Old Women* urged her, "with your next baby coming, is it not time for your little Nsia to begin to help more about the house?"

"I suppose so . . ." sighed Nsia's mother, turning away. It did not please her to ask her little girl to help — not yet!

"Childhood is so soon over!" She shrugged off the idea.

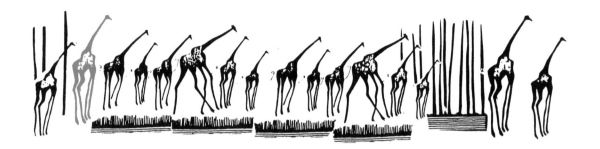

Muttering as she went, the young matron returned to her own house. Only then did she call her daughter, perhaps a little sharply:

"Nsia! Stop your running! And come here, then!"

Nsia heard her call, reminding her that her mother needed her now.

She was not a disobedient child, but in her heart, she also knew that the sharp **"Caw! Caw!"** of the wild birds called her away — the **"Splash! Splash!"** of the fish flashing in the stream below called her away — the **"Chatter! Chatter!"** of the gray monkeys perched high in the tall palms called her away — *everything* in the distance called to her, ever more strongly, all the day long!

Yet when Nsia came galloping up, with a handful of flowers, her wide eyes full of dreams, her mother sighed again and shook her head. Too well she remembered her own childhood: that feeling of being free, through endless, happy days!

Gently, then, her mother took Nsia's pointed chin in her hand.

"Nsia. Remember? Soon it is New Year's Day! We must make the new baskets for the Ceremony of Beginnings!"

Nsia nodded. She had been too young last year to understand anything but that this day was a time of good food, of family gatherings, and of much laughter.

"Everyone will be here!" her mother warned. "And the Grandfather is coming, and no wife to cook for him at all!"

Nsia grinned. Gran'pa had always liked her the best!

". . . So, Nsia," her mother was saying, "this year, with your sister away at district school, you will have to help me dig up the yams and cassava root and prepare them for the great amount of *fou-fou* I must cook."

Nsia's head drooped.

It was so different this year from the last! While she was still glad the New Year "Happy Day" was coming — she had never thought so much work went into so much fun!

Why . . . it could almost spoil it!

Her mother, seeing Nsia's bright eyes grow dim, softened.

"But that is not for a while yet, my *Flyaway Girl!* This day, I want you to run and fetch me some fresh rushes to weave the New Year's baskets!"

Nsia's eyes began to brighten.

"Where can I find them, Mama?"

"You must go to the river's edge. There you will find them!"

Her mother's voice took on a deep and serious tone.

"But listen carefully, Nsia! To make the special pattern of the baskets, I must have both dark *and* light reeds — so gather an armful of each! Then you must lay them out to dry until the sun has gone down to the top of the tallest tree."

She smiled, then, adding:

"But you can *play* until then . . ."

Nsia leaped up and grabbed her mother around the neck.

"This I will do, all by myself! I will be back . . . and with the best reeds for plaiting, Mama!"

"*Shoo!* Away, away! Go on with you, *Flyaway Girl!*"

Nsia's mother waved her off, laughing.

Then she sighed, looking after her daughter's small running figure.
"That one!" she thought. "Such a wild one! But I will bring her slowly in."
Turning away, she held her aching back.
"Just a little more time . . ." she murmured to herself.

The smell of the kitchen smoke had faded as the fresh scent of the piney woods filled Nsia's nostrils.

"Legs, legs! Get me there!"

Already Nsia's feet had carried her away from the compound, past the broom-clean earthen yard with the fresh, shining red coffee berries spread into a big circle to dry out in the tropic sun until they turned a good brown color.

Nsia ran by her Uncle Ahoud's field, where the men separated the sorghum from the stalks and the women carried away great loads of the grain on their heads.

But when Nsia ran free like this, her eyes were always fixed on the blue beyond, on the mountains that rose far above the thatched roofs and above the sunlit crowns of the tallest trees.

And sometimes she wanted to run so fast, she sang,

"Arms, arms! Fly me there!"

Nsia always hoped that, maybe, if she spread her arms like wings, she could *fly* to the tops of those high mountains . . . and then she could look down upon the whole, wide world!

"Only an eagle," Nsia said to herself, "flying very high, could see so much!"

She wanted to be like that eagle — flying free — traveling high on the rivers of air in the sky — on outspread wings — the same rivers of air that blew the clouds in the sky — and could blow and bend the tallest trees down and make the millet stalks rustle and toss . . .

"I would be *Flyaway Girl,* for real, then!" Nsia thought. "I could fly way beyond. Why . . . I'd fly over all the widest rivers in Africa . . . even the *Niger!*"

River! The rushes! She had almost forgotten her promise!

Nsia would have to forget about flying for now.

"Feet, feet! Carry me there!"

And they did.

Suddenly Nsia's toes curled with delight! She had just felt a soft coolness: the dusty feet that had carried her so far sank gratefully into the cool, moist clay at the water's edge.

She was at the river's bank! The rushes must be nearby . . .

Soon Nsia had gathered an armful of light-colored reeds and she laid them on the bank. But she could not seem to find the dark-colored ones her mother had asked for . . .

As she moved along the river's edge, searching, struggling ever deeper into the water itself, the wind seemed to follow her through the leaves and bulrushes, with an almost musical sound, and Nsia thought she heard a voice singing in the wind:

> *"Listen to things! Wise Little Woman!*
> *Hear the voice of the water . . .*

> *"Listen to the wind*
> *To the sighing of the reeds . . .*
> *To the running and sleeping waters."*

Nsia caught her breath, saying to herself,
"Heart, heart! Be strong now!"
Then Nsia turned around, and seeing no one, called out shakily,
"Who's there?"
The softly whispered sounds blew by her ear:

> *"Listen to the ancestors breathing*
> *In the trembling of the leaves*
> *In the water that runs*
> *In the worn rock."*

Nsia crouched, trembling, in the shallow water.
What could she believe? Was someone tricking her? Whose voice was this?

> *"We are the ancestor spirits*
> *Protecting you.*
> *Hear us now and always . . ."*

Nsia remembered her Gran'ma had told her that ancestor spirits protected their home. But here — at the river's edge?

Again, the answer came:

"In the river, in the trees
In the home
Each day we are with you
Binding all to life.
. . . And to one another!

We are not gone
We are in the log burning
We are in the woman's ear
Answering the child's cry . . ."

Standing up bravely, Nsia quavered:

"Then maybe . . . could you help me? . . . To — to find the dark reeds for the sacred baskets?"

As Nsia trembled, waiting, the answer came, softly:

> *"Wise Little Woman, listen!*
> *To the sighing in the darkness . . .*
> *The darkness that lightens*
> *The darkness that darkens . . .*
>
> *And in the running and*
> *The sleeping waters . . .*
> *There, close as touch*
> *You will find the dark grasses."*

Nsia took a deep breath, standing where she was, knee-deep in water and reeds . . . and closed her eyes, to listen better.

In the red darkness behind her eyelids, she could hear the birds' ***"Chirp!"*** and ***"Coo!"*** and the crickets' ***"Crik! Crik!"*** She heard the crisp ***"Rustle!"*** of leaves high above her head and the cheerful gurgle of water, ***"Lu-lu! Lu-lu!"*** as it passed by . . . and the soft ***"Sh-s-whee-e"*** of the wind, reaching out to touch her face — tickling her!

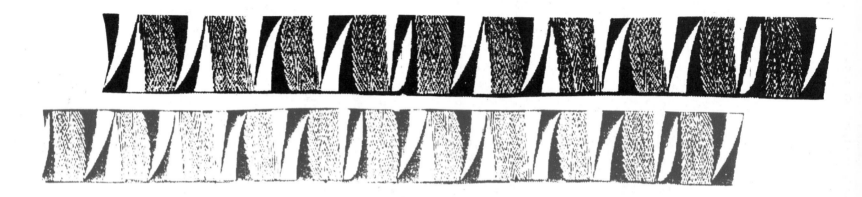

Nsia opened her eyes. A tall bulrush had leaned forward to stroke her face! Now this was a darker reed, surely! And it stood among many others just as dark, right at the river's edge!

The spirits had shared this gift with her, she knew now.

And as she quickly gathered an armful of dark rushes to go with the lighter ones, Nsia whispered, "Thank you!" to each one.

After laying them out as her mother had told her, Nsia had time to play. But instead, she sat on the banks of the river and thought and thought . . .

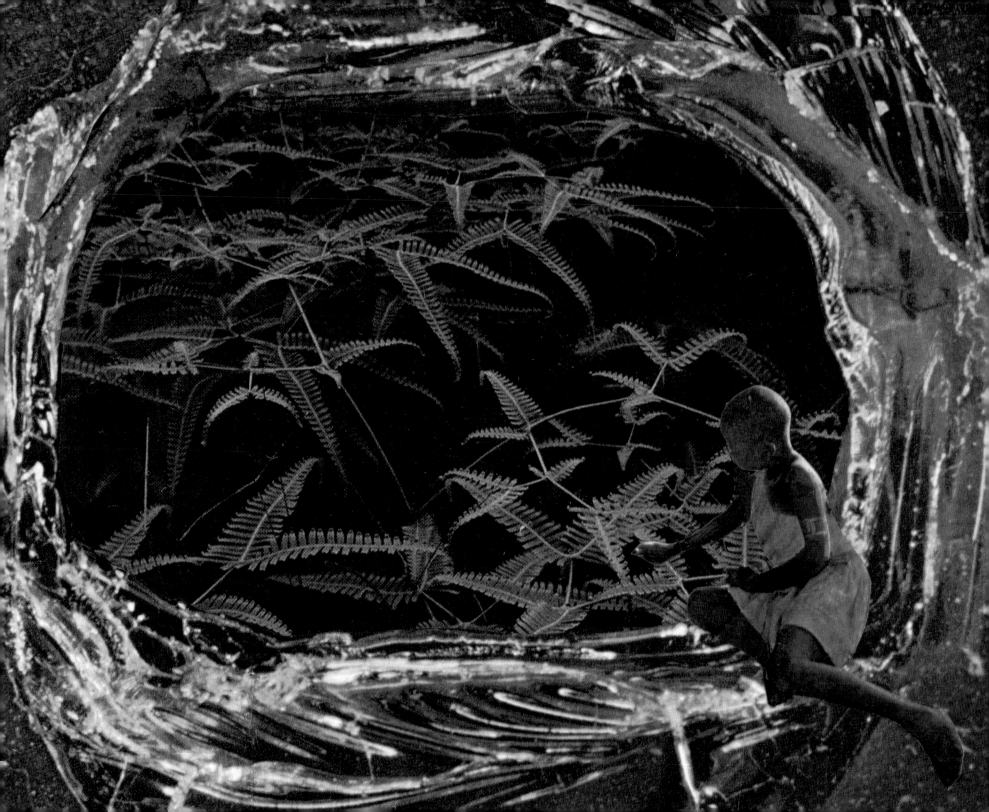

By the time she looked up, Nsia saw the low red ball of the sun flickering in the heart of a distant tree! She quickly gathered up all the reeds, now firm and dry.

Hugging the rushes close to her chest, Nsia thought she heard the wind whispering softly:

> *"Wise Little Woman!*
> *It was time for you*
> *To be ready to hold*
> *To be ready to listen . . ."*

"Wise Little Woman?" she thought to herself. . . . "Maybe I could be . . . !"

Then, as she ran home, almost flying, Nsia laughed out loud, saying, *"Legs, legs! Carry me home!"*
And they did!

JE   Grifalconi, Ann   7/93
     Flyaway girl